Lily's Apple

Story by Annette Smith

Illustrations by Samantha Asri

"Lily!" said Josh.

"Come here.

Come and look at the ants!"

"No," said Lily.

"I am not going

to look at the ants."

"Come on, Lily," said Josh.

"Come and look at the ants."

Lily looked at the ants.

The ants ran and ran.

"Oh, no!" said Lily.

"Look at my apple, Josh.

The ants are on my apple!"

"The ants are hungry,"

said Josh.

"I am hungry, too,"

said Lily.

"Here you are Lily,"

said Josh.

"Here is my apple."

"Thank you, Josh,"

said Lily.